It's See You Later, Not Goodbye

A Children's Story of Love, Loss and Coping

Catherine Fish and Roger Jeffries

It's See You Later, Not Goodbye
Copyright © 2022 by Catherine Fish and Roger Jeffries

All rights reserved. No part of this publication may be reproduced, distributed, or transmitted in any form or by any means, including photocopying, recording, or other electronic or mechanical methods, without the prior written permission of the author, except in the case of brief quotations embodied in critical reviews and certain other non-commercial uses permitted by copyright law.

Tellwell Talent
www.tellwell.ca

ISBN
978-0-2288-7738-7 (Hardcover)
978-0-2288-7737-0 (Paperback)

To the children of the world and their courage
and strength to grow through grief.

Table of Contents

Who is Ollie? Who is Grandpup? 1

Grandpup and Ollie Hear the Bad News 7

Ollie Doesn't Want to Believe the News 9

Ollie Struggles with His Feelings 11

Ollie Tries to Make a Deal 17

Ollie Feels Sad 21

Ollie Accepts Grandpup is Dying 25

Questions for Discussion 32

Resources for Support 33

A Few Words from the Author 34

Who is Ollie? Who is Grandpup?

   This is the story of two dogs. One is young and one is old. The young dog is named Ollie and the old dog, Oliver. Ollie calls him Grandpup because he is Ollie's grandfather.
   It pleases Grandpup that he and his grandson look so much alike. Both have light brown fur except for the black fur that covers their backs and sides, much like a saddle. And oddly enough, both have one blue eye and one green eye. But what pleases Grandpup the most is that Ollie's right ear is bent halfway down just like his own. It is no surprise that they get along so well.

Most days, they enjoy taking a long walk in the park where they like to collect things. They've picked up brightly colored stones, acorns and even colorful bird feathers. In fact, Grandpup still wears the shiny silver bell on his green and white collar that he found one lucky day long ago, when he was just a puppy himself. Ollie and Grandpup keep all of the treasures they find in a special place they call their "memory box." They hide the box in a corner of the doghouse that they share.

They love each other very much and have fun talking, playing and joking around. But life is not all fun and games, and Ollie has a lot to learn about the dog world. Lucky for Ollie, Grandpup is a great teacher.

Grandpup has been teaching Ollie the doggy "dos and don'ts." He has tried to convince Ollie that cats are not so bad but, given the chance, Ollie still likes to chase a stray cat up a tree. Both Grandpup and Ollie agree that a stinky skunk is something to be left alone and for good reason. Some animals should be avoided! One time, Ollie's friend Shawna tried to play with a porcupine. Apparently, porcupines do not like to play with dogs. Shawna ended up with a bunch of sharp quills stuck in her snout that had to be removed by the dog doctor, and she couldn't smell or play for a whole week!

Sadly, Grandpup knows his days of spending time with Ollie and sharing his old dog wisdom are coming to an end. He is getting old and has not been feeling well. He is just plain tired out most of the time. He knows he should go and see the dog doctor before he says anything to Ollie.

Grandpup and Ollie Hear the Bad News

It was Monday afternoon when Ollie heard the jingling of Grandpup's silver bell on his collar and knew he was near. Ollie peeked out of the doghouse and saw Grandpup walking slowly down the sidewalk, coming home from the doctor's office. Ollie raced out of the doghouse.

"Grandpup! What did the doctor tell you? What's the problem?" called Ollie as he jumped up and down wagging his tail. "Good news I hope."

Grandpup joined Ollie and they walked slowly back home to their doghouse. Grandpup said in a calm, gentle voice, "Ollie my boy, what the doctor had to say was not good news nor was it really bad news. He said that I am getting old and that it's natural for everything and everybody to wear out over time. I just have to take it easy. You know, I'm fourteen years old, and in people years, that means I'm seventy."

Ollie Doesn't Want to Believe the News

It was a sunny afternoon and Ollie felt like playing. He wanted Grandpup to run around the yard with him and chase some squirrels. Ollie spotted Grandpup lying under a maple tree and excitedly ran to him. "Grandpup, get up! Let's go run—you can chase me first."

Grandpup looked up at Ollie and squinted into the bright sunlight. "I'm sorry Ollie, I just don't have the energy today. I need to rest for a bit. Remember, the doctor told me to take it easy."

"I don't believe what the doctor said," insisted Ollie. "I think the doctor is wrong. You know that collie down the street from us? His grandpup was old and didn't feel well, but now he is better. Besides, I had a dream last night and in it you were as good as new."

Grandpup tried to reason with Ollie saying that all good things must come to an end with time, but Ollie would not listen. He did not like what he was hearing. Ollie had always been a happy, fun-loving puppy and now he felt different. At times he became angry and upset. He didn't like these feelings, but he couldn't help it.

Ollie Struggles with His Feelings

Early one morning as the sun rose over the doghouse, Grandpup called to Ollie. "Ollie get out here." Ollie was fast asleep in their doghouse.

Ollie appeared at the doghouse door rubbing the sleep from his eyes. "What's up Grandpup?" Ollie yawned.

With a stern voice, Grandpup demanded, "How did all of these holes get dug in the yard?"

Ollie approached with his tail between his legs. "Before we went to bed last night, I felt like doing something bad, so I dug some holes."

Grandpup continued, "And what about the flower garden? It looks like a tornado came through here. You and I planted those flowers last spring."

"I know," said Ollie. "I'm sorry. I guess I tore up those flowers because it made me feel better at the time. I just had a lot of feelings to get out."

"I think I know what you mean Ollie. It is normal and okay to feel angry after the bad news we talked about yesterday. But it's how you show it that counts. Destroying something is not a good way to show anger."

"Well, what are good ways?" asked Ollie, genuinely interested.

Grandpup thought for a moment and replied: "Anger is kind of like the wind. It blows in and it blows out. There are things we can do to help anger blow on through, like run around the yard or play with our friends. Being active helps us feel better. You also can talk to me about what you're feeling, because chances are, I might be feeling the same way. Sometimes it feels good to know you are not the only one feeling angry. Another way might be to draw a picture that shows how you are feeling And, since you've already dug the holes, how about we plant some acorns from our memory box? Then we can cover them up with dirt and wait for the trees to grow."

Ollie cocked his head to the side and thought for a moment. He really didn't feel like filling the holes back up with dirt but doing it together with Grandpup might be fun. So, together they planted their acorns and replanted the flowers, and Ollie was right. They did have fun. And Grandpup was also right. Ollie did feel better. But then Ollie had an idea. He wanted to make a deal with Grandpup.

Ollie Tries to Make a Deal

Ollie realized that Grandpup might die soon. Ollie did not want to say goodbye to him. He had not given up hope that Grandpup would always be his best friend and that maybe Grandpup could do something to stay around longer.

Each was lying in his own bed one evening when Ollie rolled over toward Grandpup and said, "I don't want you to die Grandpup. How about we make a deal?"

"What kind of deal are you talking about?" asked Grandpup.

"My deal is this," replied Ollie. "I know you don't feel like eating all of your dog food every day. Sometimes I don't like the food we get, and I bury half of mine in the backyard and say that I ate all of it. From now on, I'll eat all of mine if you eat all of yours. Then you will stay strong and live for a long, long time."

Grandpup replied in a disappointed tone, "What? You've been burying your food? That is very wasteful Ollie. You had better just eat all of yours, and I will try to eat a little more of mine."

Displeasing Grandpup made Ollie feel a little bad and sorry to the bone. He decided he would eat all of his dog food just like Grandpup asked.

The following day, Ollie suggested another deal. "Grandpup, you know that orange cat from down the street that keeps hanging around here? You've told me a thousand times to stop chasing him out of our yard because he causes no trouble. Here's the deal: if you pay no attention to what that quack dog doctor told you about getting old, then I will ask that snoopy orange cat if he would like to move into our house with us."

Grandpup chuckled because he was quite certain the cat would say, "No, thank you" to Ollie's offer to move in. Grandpup was a wise old dog. He understood the real reason Ollie was wanting to make a deal. Ollie loved his Grandpup so much and was having a hard time with the thought of losing him and having to say goodbye. Ollie thought maybe he could change the natural way of things if he behaved himself. Grandpup looked lovingly at Ollie and tried to explain what that natural way is.

"My dear Ollie boy, there is a natural flow to everything in life. For example, think about the green leaves on a tree. As time goes on, they change to red, orange and yellow. As the leaves get older, they dry up and turn brown; they fall off the branches and onto the ground where we enjoy jumping and playing in them. A puppy is very much the same. As time goes on, it grows to be an adult dog and then an old, wise dog. When the old dog's body wears out, its soul moves on and leaves the body behind. When the time comes for your soul to move on Ollie, we'll be reunited once again. So, you see, it's not "goodbye." It's more like "see you later."

Ollie could almost understand that. He liked the thought that his soul would be with Grandpup's soul one day. But still, he became saddened at the thought of Grandpup getting older and older like the dying leaves on a tree.

Ollie Feels Sad

As time went on, Grandpup grew a little older and weaker. Ollie had times when he felt very sad. Occasionally at mealtime, Ollie ate less of his favorite food as he just didn't feel much like eating. There were days he didn't even feel like going on a walk or playing with friends. He would rather just lie in their doghouse. Grandpup had noticed Ollie wasn't his usual happy puppy self lately. His tail, which used to always be wagging, now drooped to the ground. Grandpup felt it was time to share some more of that dog wisdom that only old dogs knew.

"Hey Ollie," Grandpup called as he stood outside of the doghouse. "Come out in the sunshine and talk with me for a while."

Ollie slowly crawled out of the dark doghouse into the bright, warm sunshine. He covered his blue and green eyes with his paw as they adjusted to the brightness and replied, "Okay, I'm coming Grandpup."

"Ollie, I've noticed you've been sad, and I want you to know that you are not alone. When I think about dying, sometimes I feel sad too. It's okay to feel sad. I'd like to share something that I have always found to be true."

"What is it?" Ollie asked.

"I have found when we feel sad, there are things we can do to help ourselves feel better."

"Like what?" wondered Ollie.

"Well, playing outside in the fresh air and sunshine makes your spirit happy. Did you notice that when we went on walks in the park, we felt so energized and we smiled and laughed a lot? Each day, you should try to get out of the doghouse and play for a bit, even if you don't feel like it. Also, eating your dog food, drinking water and getting a good night's sleep will help your body stay strong."

"And do you want to know the most powerful thing you can do to feel better?"

"Oh yes, Grandpup," Ollie said quickly.

"Help others out whenever you can Ollie. Helping others makes your spirit very, very happy." Ollie thought about this for a moment. He could feel Grandpup was sharing something quite special with him.

Ollie did as Grandpup suggested even though he didn't fully understand or feel much like doing it. Each time he left the yard for his walk, Grandpup would call out, "Keep your tail up Ollie." This always made Ollie smile a little bit and he really did feel better when he followed Grandpup's advice.

As the weeks passed, Grandpup became less active and stayed in their doghouse much of the time. He ate very little of his food but did drink from his water bowl that Ollie always made certain was filled to the brim. Ollie also kept a blanket on Grandpup to keep him warm. It made Ollie feel good to help Grandpup.

Ollie Accepts Grandpup is Dying

One afternoon, Grandpup lay down just outside of the doghouse to feel the warm afternoon sun on his fur. Ollie went into the doghouse, brought out the memory box and lay down beside him. He opened the box, and they admired the many treasures.

Ollie looked up at Grandpup and said softly, "Grandpup, I'm really going to miss you and the good ol' days."

"And I will miss you too, Ollie. We have a lot of great memories, don't we kiddo? Remember when you used to chase your tail? Round and round you'd go, and never once did you catch it! Or the times you hid your bone and I dug it up and hid it somewhere else and you couldn't find it?"

Ollie said with a grin, "You thought that was a good joke—but I didn't. Then I got back at you by burying your glasses!"

"And of course," continued Grandpup, "remember all of our adventures on our walks and the many treasures we found for the memory box."

Ollie smiled. His heart felt full of love for Grandpup. "Grandpup, even though I will miss you, I know your soul will be in a happy place, and I will be okay. I promise to remember everything you have taught me."

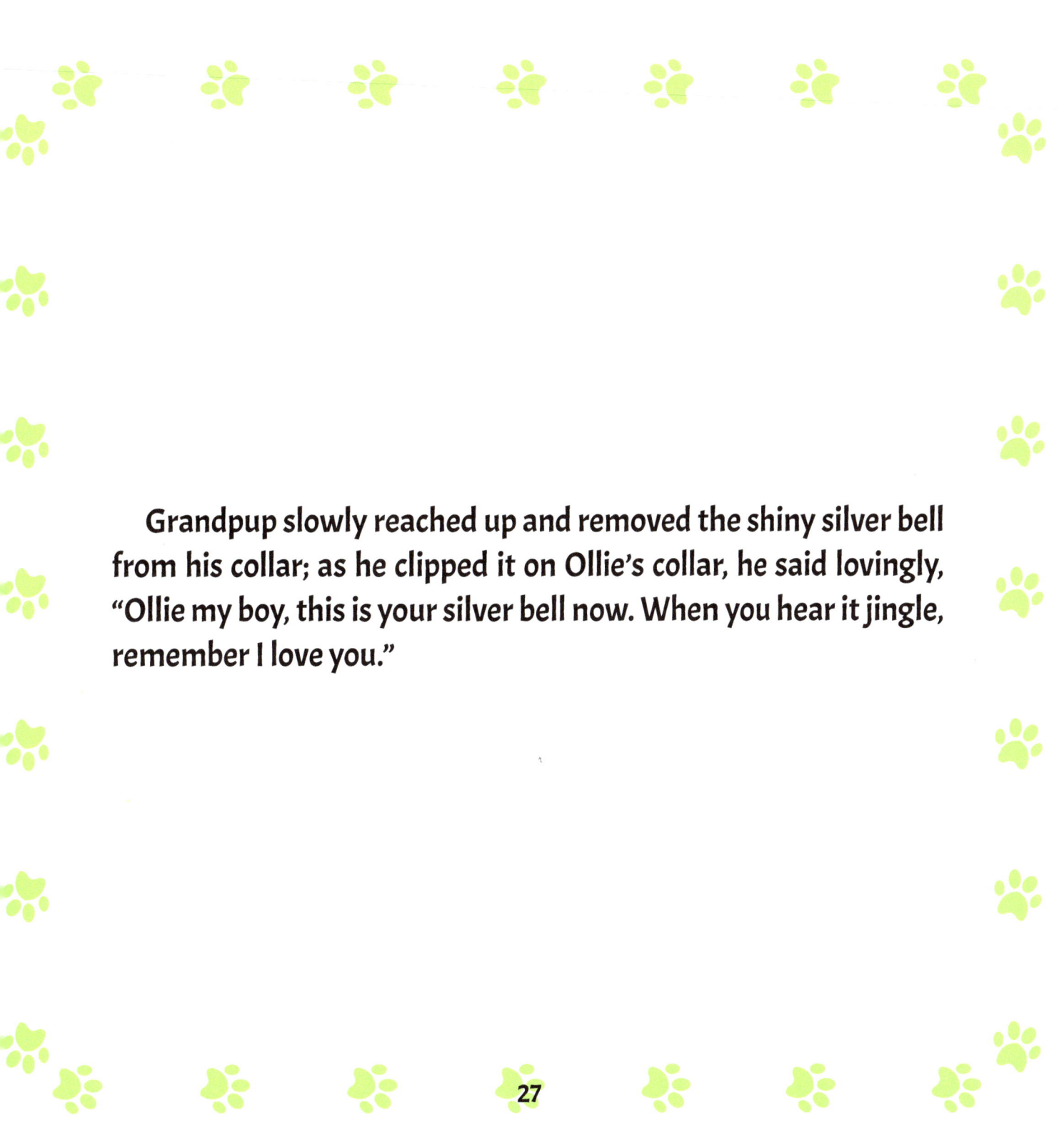

Grandpup slowly reached up and removed the shiny silver bell from his collar; as he clipped it on Ollie's collar, he said lovingly, "Ollie my boy, this is your silver bell now. When you hear it jingle, remember I love you."

The following morning, Grandpup did not wake up. He had died peacefully during the night lying on his bed. Ollie walked slowly to him and gently laid his head on Grandpup's furry shoulder and whispered:

My grandpup is special,
My grandpup is kind,
A wise dog like you
Is a very rare find.

We played and we ran,
And whistled a tune,
Spent our days in the sun,
And howled at the moon.

I promise dear Grandpup,
To make you proud,
Always trying my best,
And not barking too loud.

You filled me with love,
Gave what I needed to grow,
When I hear your bell jingle,
My grateful heart will glow.

I will miss you my grandpup,
I might even cry,
But I know it's not forever,
It's *see you later*, not *goodbye*.

Questions for Discussion

1. Why do you think Ollie did not want to believe his grandfather was sick? (denial)

2. Ollie tore up their flower garden when he was angry. Can you think of a time when you felt angry? If you can, what did you do? (anger)

3. Ollie told Grandpup that he would eat all of his dog food if Grandpup would eat all of his. Have you ever tried to make a deal with someone? For example, have you said, "If you do this, I'll do that?" (bargaining)

4. Ollie felt sad when he realized that Grandpup was getting older and not feeling well. We have all felt sad at times. What makes you feel sad? (depression)

5. Even though Ollie knew Grandpup was dying, he was strong and brave and told Grandpup that he knew Grandpup's soul would be in a happy place. Have you ever had to do something that you did not want to do but you did it because it was the right thing to do? If you did, what was it and what did you do? (acceptance)

Resources for Support

1. National Alliance for Children's Grief (NACG)
https://childrengrieve.org/find-support

2. The Dougy Center: The National Grief Center for Children & Families
https://www.dougy.org

3. Rainbows for All Children
https://rainbows.org

A Few Words from the Author

Dear Reader,

    Thank you for finding this little book! I hope you enjoy reading it as much as Roger and I enjoyed writing it. I love knowing the backstory on books—where the idea came from and how the book came to be. It is no surprise I'm sharing the backstory of this book because it is another story in itself!

    I am a hospice nurse at the community hospital in Owosso, Michigan. My co-author, Roger, is my hospice client. Prior to our meeting, Roger had been in the hospital with heart issues that were not going to improve, and his doctor had recommended hospice services for extra support and end-of-life care. Roger was not thrilled with the idea of hospice and someone coming into his home to check on him. He lived independently and valued his privacy highly. However, after a few visits, we realized we had many things in common. For example, both of our spouses had died of cancer. I had lost my husband Carmen fifteen years earlier and Roger's wife JoAnn had passed ten years prior. We are also both U.S. Navy veterans. Over time, Roger began to look forward to my visits and slowly, a dear friendship grew.

    One day, we were discussing the novel that Roger and JoAnn had written, and I mentioned I had always wanted to write a children's book. Roger began asking a lot of questions about my ideas for the book, which made me think perhaps it was time to actually write it.

    As a hospice nurse, I discovered a need for children's books that address the subject of death and dying. They can be used as a tool to facilitate conversation, exploration and emotional support for children who have experienced loss.

After I made the decision to write the book, I asked Roger if he would mentor me through the writing process as he was a published author. He said, "Yes!" and then became a man on a mission. We scheduled writing sessions to work on the book. The first day, I walked into his home and Roger said, "Come on—writers write!" Well, on my first official day as a writer, I sat down and . . . nothing. I had writer's block! This was not encouraging. Thankfully, at the following sessions, the creative energy and collaboration naturally flowed, so well in fact that we ended up writing the story together.

I feel so much gratitude for the beautiful friendship that developed between Roger and me during the process of creating this book. There was a lot of joy and laughter, and of course, some mild disagreements. Roger was the one who made sure we kept moving the project forward.

We each grew in our own way. Writing the book became a tool for Roger to explore his own thoughts and feelings about death and dying and being a hospice client. Similarly, it became a means for me to process the grief I was feeling after the passing of my dad the previous year.

On a side note, Roger is a Michigan State University fan and that is why Grandpup's collar is green and white. Ollie's collar is navy blue with an anchor as a shout-out to our Navy comrades.

My hope is that you find this story both enjoyable and helpful in the exploration of your own experience with loss.

Best wishes,

Catherine

Acknowledgements

To Megs, my one and only child. You are my most significant other. The way you live your life with love, light and passion inspires me every day. Together we rise! I love, love, love you.

To my co-author Roger, oh my gosh, how to put this into words? When the right person comes along at the right time and in the right place, magic happens and it for darn sure happened with us my dear friend! This book would not have happened without you. Thank you for being my mentor and my friend, and for sharing your many stories from a life well lived with your forever bride JoAnn and your family. You've left an impression on my heart that will last a lifetime.

To my mom, you were the first to love me. Your love, support and hours of prayers have always been so appreciated. Thank you for instilling in me the belief that "I can." I love you more than words can say.

To my dad, if you were still here, I know you would be proud and would especially enjoy the poem at the end of the story as you were a bit of a poet yourself. I love you and will most definitely *see you later!*

To Rosta, thank you for the many years of love, laughter and dear friendship. You've helped me transform the pain from loss into inner strength and power. Words cannot express my gratitude… much love always to you and sweet Koda-bear.

To family and friends, thank you for your support and for encouraging me to follow a dream.

To my Memorial Healthcare Hospice team, thank you for being the beautiful souls that you are and for creating a loving and supportive space that enables each of us to give our best to clients and their families. You make a difference!

To our illustrator i Cenizal, your talent is greatly appreciated. You pictorially brought this story to life!

Catherine Fish was born and raised in Owosso, Michigan. She is a registered nurse and holds a Master's degree in Advanced Holistic Nursing. She served in the U.S. Navy Nurse Corps at the beginning of her career and spent the next twenty-five years living in South Carolina and North Carolina engaged in various nursing specialties before returning to her roots to help her family care for her father who was ill. She has one child, Megs and lovely daughter-in-law Amanda, who share their home with Oliver, the puppy who inspired the character of Ollie. Catherine enjoys activities that support mind, body and spirit balance such as meditation, hiking, biking, tai chi, cooking and building connections with family and friends. She is a spiritual seeker and has always felt a passion for growth and knowledge.

Roger, Catherine

Ollie Fishwell

Roger Jeffries makes his home in Corunna, Michigan where he and his late wife, JoAnn, enjoyed fifty-two years of married happiness. They co-authored and published nine books on speech and language development for therapists, teachers and parents. They also wrote and published a mystery novel. Roger and JoAnn traveled extensively to all seven continents, seventy-six countries of the world and forty-eight of the fifty United States. Roger holds a Master's degree from Michigan State University in Guidance and Counseling and in Social Work and a Bachelor's degree in Secondary Education. He devoted his entire professional career to working with and for the benefit of children in the public-school setting. He was a teacher, a guidance counselor, a school social worker and a director of special education. He is also a U.S. Navy veteran. Roger has a wonderful family and is enjoying retirement under the watchful eye and care of his hospice nurse Cathy. In this book, Ollie's friend Shawna is based on Roger's loyal dog and companion that recently died at an old age of cancer.

Shawna

Printed in the USA
CPSIA information can be obtained
at www.ICGtesting.com
LVHW071120011124
795435LV00033B/329